Joseph T. Smith

A Discourse on the Life and Character of the Rev. Henry V.D. Johns

Anatiposi

Joseph T. Smith

A Discourse on the Life and Character of the Rev. Henry V.D. Johns

Reprint of the original.

1st Edition 2023 | ISBN: 978-3-38230-792-9

Anatiposi Verlag is an imprint of Outlook Verlagsgesellschaft mbH.

Verlag (Publisher): Outlook Verlag GmbH, Zeilweg 44, 60439 Frankfurt, Deutschland
Vertretungsberechtigt (Authorized to represent): E. Roepke, Zeilweg 44, 60439 Frankfurt, Deutschland
Druck (Print): Books on Demand GmbH, In de Tarpen 42, 22848 Norderstedt, Deutschland

A

DISCOURSE

ON THE

LIFE AND CHARACTER

OF THE

Rev. HENRY V. D. JOHNS, D. D.

LATE RECTOR OF EMANUEL CHURCH, BALTIMORE,

By JOSEPH T. SMITH,

Pastor of the 2d Presbyterian Church,

MAY 22, 1859.

———————

Second Edition with an Appendix.

———————

BALTIMORE:

PUBLISHED BY THE MARYLAND TRACT SOCIETY,

Tract House, 73 Fayette-st.

JOHN W. WOODS, PRINTER.

1859.

The circumstances connected with the publication of this Memorial of Affection are sufficiently explained by the following extracts and correspondence:

TRACT HOUSE,
BALTIMORE, *May 3d*, 1859.

At a meeting of the Executive Committee of the Maryland Tract Society, this day held, it was, on motion of Mr. A. M. CARTER, unanimously resolved, that the Rev. JOSEPH T. SMITH be requested to preach a Sermon commemorative of the Life and Character of our late lamented President, and that arrangements be made for its delivery at as early a day as may be convenient.

Extract from the Minutes,
S. B. BRACKETT,
Rec. Secretary.

TRACT HOUSE,
BALTIMORE, *May 24th*, 1859.

At a special meeting of the Managers of the Maryland Tract Society, this day convened, it was, on motion, unanimously resolved, that this Board hereby express our very great gratification with the Sermon commemorative of the life and character of our late lamented President, the Rev. H. V. D. JOHNS, D. D.; that we tender our cordial thanks to the Rev. Dr. SMITH for the service rendered us, and that we request a copy for publication.

Extract from the Minutes,
S. B. BRACKETT,
Rec. Secretary.

BALTIMORE, *May 25th*, 1859.

Rev. J. T. SMITH, D. D.,

    Rev. and Dear Sir,

        In presenting you the foregoing action of the Managers of our Tract Society, allow us to assure you of our earnest personal concurrence in the sentiments expressed, and our hope that you will see no objection to furnishing a copy for publication.   Very truly, yours,

        In behalf of the Board,

          J. W. M. WILLIAMS,
          G. C. M. ROBERTS,
          ELIAS HEINER,
          E. Y. REESE,
          HALSEY DUNNING,
          A. M. CARTER,
          W. K. MERRITT,
          WILLIAM BRIDGES.

BALTIMORE, *May 25th*, 1859.

GENTLEMEN :

    The Discourse "on the Life and Character of Dr. JOHNS," a copy of which you request for publication, was prepared for an audience of whose cordial sympathy in everything my heart prompted me to say of him I was sure. I fear that it may not be suited for the press, or for the hands of readers who did not know our dear friend and brother. I do not feel at liberty, however, under the circumstances, to refuse your request, and the manuscript is herewith placed at your disposal.

        Respectfully and fraternally,

          Yours, &c.

          JOSEPH T. SMITH.

To Rev. J. W. M. WILLIAMS,
    Rev. Dr. G. C. M. ROBERTS,
    Rev. Dr. E. HEINER,
      and others.

NOTE BY COMMITTEE OF PUBLICATION.

The Sermon, it may be proper to add, was delivered in the Central Presbyterian Church, Rev. Thos. E. Peck, D. D., Pastor, on Sabbath P. M., May 22d, to one of the largest assemblages ever convened in this city on any similar occasion, the vast church being filled to its utmost capacity, and multitudes being unable to gain admittance.

The services, which were of the deepest solemnity and tenderness, were also a beautiful illustration of Christian union, ministers of the Gospel connected with eight different denominations participating in the exercises.

DISCOURSE.

FOR TO ME TO LIVE IS CHRIST, AND TO DIE IS GAIN.—Philippians i, 21.

THESE words were penned by the Apostle while a prisoner in Rome, and just upon the eve of his trial. They may be regarded as his last words—the deliberate testimony of a Christian minister, uttered while standing upon the border-line between life and death, calmly surveying both. In writing to the Philippians, who seem to have been to him what the family of Bethany was to the Master, the Apostle admits them to the inmost secrecies of his soul in that solemn hour. He tells them how he is "in a strait betwixt two"—having "a desire to depart, and be with Christ," yet wishing still "to abide with them in the flesh;" longing for his rest and his reward, yet willing still to labor and to suffer. And then, in the volume-embracing words of our text, he sums up his whole estimate of those two tremendous facts—Life and Death. "For to me to live is Christ,

and to die is gain." As if he had said, "I live, yet
not I, but Christ, who is my life, liveth in me; and
the life that I now live, I live by Faith in the Son of
God. I live not unto myself, but unto Him who
loved me, and gave Himself for me. Christ is the
beginning and the end; the centre and the circum-
ference; the all in all of my being. I live for no
selfish or secular end; for nothing which men seek
after, or the world can bestow. Accounting my
life as but a season and an opportunity for doing good,
I live only to labor for Christ, and to fill up what is
behind of His sufferings, and I am willing to live
for Christ. But 'to die is gain'—infinite and everlasting gain. I shrink not from the approach of the
last enemy, for to me Christ hath abolished Death,
and put these words of triumph in my mouth: O!
Death, where is thy sting? O! Grave, where is thy
victory? The sting of Death is sin, and the strength
of sin is the law; but thanks be unto God who giveth
us the victory, through our Lord Jesus Christ.
And then Faith looks beyond and above. Henceforth there is laid up for me a crown of righteousness. In my Father's house are many mansions, and
Christ has gone before to prepare a place for me, and
it will be gain for me to be at home—forever at home
—with Him."

Our detailed exposition of the text will be found in
the life and death of that man of God, who has just
been removed from among us to join the great cloud
of witnesses above. We undertake this service as a

feeble tribute to departed worth—as a new testimony
to the grace of God towards His servants, in life and
in death—and as a fresh incentive to renewed diligence in the duties of our high calling. It is not of
the man we would speak. but of the disciple. It is
not the man we would glorify, but the grace of God
which was "exceeding abundant" towards him. And
our design in this service will be altogether frustrated
if it do not redound to the praise of the glory of
God's grace.

The Rev. HENRY VAN DYKE JOHNS, D.D., was
born in Newcastle, Delaware, on the 23d day of
October, in the year of our Lord, 1803. He was the
descendant of an old Maryland family, founded by
Richard Johns, who emigrated from England and
settled in Calvert County in 1717. He was the son
of the late Judge Kensey Johns, and brother of the
late Chancellor of Delaware, and of the present Bishop
of Virginia. He inherited from his ancestors the rich-
est of all legacies—the blessing entailed from father
to son upon the generations of those who fear God.
A child of the covenant, and sealed with the seal of
the covenant in infancy. his character was formed and
unfolded amidst the hallowed influences of a Christian
home.

His collegiate education was commenced at Princeton, while the college, under the Presidency of Dr.
Green, was visited with that memorable revival which

gave so many ministers to the Church, and baptized them with so large a measure of the Spirit. The subject of religious impressions from his earliest childhood, these were deepened by contact with the revival spirit, and especially by the ministrations of the late Dr. Archibald Alexander The following incident, connected with this period of his life, is from the pen of Dr. James W. Alexander. "The first person with whom I ever talked freely concerning the infinite concerns of my soul, was Henry V. D. Johns, and he has told me that a like remark was true of himself. It was in Nassau Hall, then the principal edifice of Princeton College, and in No. 27 in the 'second entry,' a locality fresh in the memory of old Nassovians. We were boys of sixteen, though I was about to commence Bachelor of Arts. Such conversations begin one scarcely knows how ; in a short time we had unbosomed ourselves to one another, and entered upon a close and tender friendship, which, I trust in God, is never to cease. During the days in which Henry was under the work of the law, and humbly doubting whether, indeed, he had attained to justification or not, he used to walk in the grove behind the college, which, alas, with other forest shades of my boyhood, has long since vanished away. As he strayed, musing, his eye was attracted by a small folded paper upon the ground ; this he picked up, and afterwards showed to me ; it contained these words : 'And they that are Christ's have crucified the flesh with the affections and lusts.' Gal. v, 24.

'*Try yourself by this.*' This incident made a deep
impression on us both, conveying to our apprehensions, at that time, something of the supernatural.
We have talked it over in later years, and there is
reason to believe that it had a moulding influence on
Johns' experience and life." Under these blessed
influences the seed, sown and watered through so
many years, ripened in his heart into its glorious har-
vest. Here he received that Baptism of the Spirit
which made him the Evangelist he was.

Partly from considerations of health, and partly
from the disturbed state of the college during the last
years of Dr. Green's administration, he removed from
Princeton, and was graduated at Union, in 1823.
Immediately after his graduation he commenced his
studies for the ministry, first with his brother, and
then at the General Theological Seminary, N. Y.
He was ordained a Deacon in the Protestant Episcopal
Church by the venerated Bishop White, in Emanuel
Church, Newcastle, Delaware, in 1826, and a Presby-
ter by Bishop Chase, in St. John's Church, Washington, D. C., in 1828. Soon after he received an ap-
pointment as Chaplain in the Navy, and was assigned
to the vessel which was to convey Lafayette back
from his last visit to the United States to his native
land. After prayerful deliberation, however, he was
led to devote his life to the pastorate. And in a little
unfurnished hall, with a rude pine table for his pulpit,
he gathered and organized his first church, now
Trinity Church, in Washington. Thence he removed

to Baltimore, and ministered, for a time, to "Old
Trinity," under circumstances of great discourage-
ment. Thence he removed to Frederick, Md., and
thence, after the lapse of five years, back to Baltimore,
where he organized and served for a time St. Andrew's
Church. This church being weak and struggling with
many embarrassments, he was induced to accept a
charge in Cincinnati, where he labored with great
acceptance until 1842, when he was called to Christ
Church, Baltimore, to which he ministered until the
organization of Emanuel, in 1854, in the service of
which he died.

In asking me to sketch the character of this man of
God, so as to give the proper relief to its more prom-
inent features, you have called me to a task to which
I feel myself inadequate. My personal relations to
Dr. Johns have so endeared his memory, that I can
speak of him only with the affectionate partiality of a
son for a revered father. My personal intercourse
with him was such, that his faults, whatever they
were, were never discovered. The only portrait I can
draw of him, truthfully, must be all in light; you
must supply the shades.

I. Intellectually, he may be best characterized, perhaps, by that expressive phrase, "a well balanced
mind." His mental faculties, such as they were,
were all in a state of happy equipoise. None were
wanting, none were in excess, and all were blended
into a structure, beautiful and symmetrical as a Grecian

temple. He had not Genius, but he had many and varied Talents. He was not the Palm, gathering all its riches into its tufted top, and lifting that up to the clouds, and out of reach; he was the humbler Olive tree, covered all over with branches, laden with the choicest fruit, and bending down to the earth.

He was, through life, an indefatigable student; feeding his people with knowledge and not with wind. It was his habit to spend the earlier part of every week in reading, chiefly professional; and the latter part in arranging and elaborating his discourses, not writing, but manipulating them with his thoughts till they stood out complete and illuminated in every part before his mind's eye—scrupulously redeeming for this purpose, every fragment of time, cut up as his time always was, into fragments. His style was singularly chaste, almost classic. His language was polished, until like the clearest crystal, it transmitted without tinging or refracting the light of his thoughts. He had acquired the art, so seldom acquired, of saying exactly what he wanted to say. He was not eloquent, in the popular and profane sense of that word. He knew not, and despised to know how to make the crowd gape and applaud. He practiced no stares or starts, or mouthings or attitudenizings, or stage tricks, or pulpit impertinencies of any kind. Self-possessed, simple, solemn, he might have served for the original of Cowper's preacher.

But his chief power, and it is the highest species of power—far mightier than the strong arm, or the giant intellect, or the iron will—was the POWER OF GOODNESS. I say it deliberately, and you, who have known him so long and so well, are all witnesses, Dr. Johns approached as near perfection in moral character, as is allowed to mortals. His tastes were all elevated, his sensibilities refined, his whole nature recoiled with its very strongest instincts from the approach of anything low or base. His spirit, gentle as that of a child, loving as that of a mother, was the clear reflection of His "who was meek and lowly in heart." He was "clothed with humility," as with a garment, which only heightened while it sought to conceal his excellence. Simple and unpretentious, always ready to take the lowest place, and to esteem others better than himself; like the Master, he accounted it his highest honor to be "the servant of all." Forgetful of himself, there was nothing about him to repel the approach of the humblest; and "nothing which concerned man did he regard as foreign to himself." His sympathies were quick and warm, leading him to enter intuitively, and with his whole heart, into the feelings of others—to "rejoice with those who rejoiced and to weep with those who wept." Who ever approached him in perplexity or in sorrow and did not find him a brother indeed? O! how this large-heartedness grappled his friends to him with hooks of steel. The purity of his motives was transparent, the sincerity of his professions undoubted. And this goodness made itself felt everywhere as a mighty power. There was a majesty about it which

rebuked from its presence everything mean or un-
manly. There was an inspiration about it which im-
parted, at least a temporary, elevation, to all who
came within its reach. There was a charm about it
which extorted the homage even of the worldly and the
profane. How often has the remark been heard from
the lips of such, "I like Dr. Johns, for I believe he is
a good man." Seldom has the POWER OF GOODNESS
been more signally exemplified in any community.
The gentleness and purity which surrounded him as a
halo, were, however, far from being associated with
weakness or pusillanimity of spirit . He was firm and
inflexible, as was shown more than once in the course
of his ministerial life, where the truth was at stake.
He was always courageous for the Right—a very hero
where the glory of his Master, the success of his cause
or the liberties of his people were concerned.

But we have not yet reached "the hiding" of his
power. His Goodness was sanctified and sublimated
into Piety. His Virtues were transfigured into Graces.
He was a temple of the Holy Ghost; and the light
which shone about him was the light of Heaven.
His piety was after the earlier, apostolic standard—
healthful, genial, expansive, laborious. He was no
enthusiast, floating through dream-lands, and feeding
on visions and ecstacies. He had no revelations,
save such as were common to his brethren. The holy
things of his own heart he delighted not to drag from
their inner sanctuary, and expose to the rude gaze,
and ruder handling of the multitude. His religious

experiences were eminently sober and scriptural. His religion approved itself, as towards God, in a life of Consecration.

"All that I am and all I have
Shall be forever thine."

These words in his lips, were to be taken in their true literal import. He was pre-eminently a man of prayer. He saw Him who is invisible. He walked with God. He was often with Him on the Mount, talking with Him "as a man with his friend," till his face shone. Three times a day, it was his invariable custom, from his first entrance on the divine life, to retire for secret prayer. Every important undertaking was commenced with prayer; and in every perplexity he sought first the wisdom that cometh from above. How often when friends have gone to consult him, has he risen up and locked his study door, and said, now that we can be alone, let us pray. As towards man his religion approved itself by a life of Benevolence. He was always ready to do good. What good cause ever failed to find in him a friend and an advocate? His time, his talents, his influence, his money, all were freely employed to promote the best interests of society. Throughout his life it was his rule to devote the one-tenth of all his income to charitable uses. And so scrupulous was he in enforcing this rule upon himself. that whenever he received a present, even though trifling—a book, a wedding-fee, a basket of fruit—he put a valuation upon it, and gave the one-tenth unto the Lord. For to him "to live was Christ."

II. The gospel he preached was the gospel of the apostles and the reformers—the gospel of the articles and the homilies. His doctrinal views were clearly and distinctively evangelical; sharply distinguished on the one side from Rationalism, and on the other from Romanism. I cannot better express them than in his own language: "Holy Scripture; the sole source and rule of faith, not Scripture and tradition as its joint rule Man—a fallen and depraved being, utterly unable by his own strength to save himself; and our Lord Jesus Christ an all-sufficient and perfect Saviour. Repentance—consisting in the knowledge of sin, sorrow for sin, abandoning of sin, and turning fully unto God. Saving Faith—-the repose of the stricken soul upon the testimony of God concerning his Son Jesus Christ, our only Saviour, Mediator and Redeemer. Pardon—the direct gift of Christ to every one that believeth with the heart, with no intervention other than the truth and spirit of God, not dependent on a priestly or human agency for its certainty of reception. Justification—a free act of God, in consideration of the obedience and death of Christ, received by faith without works; 'not an inward character in man, consisting of faith as one of a catalogue of justifying graces.' Sanctification—the progressive work of the Holy Ghost, restoring the image of God in righteousness and true holiness to the soul, and thus in all scriptural obedience and Godly living, by the truth, making us new creatures in Christ Jesus. Sanctification, being a work performed within us; Justification, a work performed without us. Justification, rendering us safe in view of death and judgment; Sanctification giving us evidence that we are safe." Paul could have subscribed such a creed as that, and Luther and Cranmer, for it is the glorious gospel of the blessed God. And in proclaiming these great cardinal truths, he uttered no "uncertain sound," his silvery voice rang them out clearly and sharply, so that all must hear and none could mistake.

As a Pastor, he chiefly excelled. His great usefulness, and the almost unexampled love his people bore to him were largely attributable to his ministrations at the fireside, and in the sick chamber, and the house of mourning; his earnest personal appeals to the careless and impenitent, and his affectionate counsels to those who were asking after the "way of life."

His ministry was eminently fruitful He has left to this city three churches, free from debt, and maintaining regularly the ordinances of God's house— Emanuel Church—Emanuel Chapel, and Cranmer Chapel. The church he served, though one of the youngest, appears from the last Journal of the Protestant Episcopal Church in Maryland, to be the first in the State, in the number of its communicants, and the general evidences of pastoral usefulness. All over this city are those who honor him, and mourn for him as their spiritual father. And in every place where he has ministered, many—how many, the judgment alone can declare—have been given him, and will yet be given him, as "seals of his ministry."

Dr. Johns was earnestly, and honestly, and upon mature conviction, attached to the distinctive polity of his own church, as, in his view, most closely conformed to the apostolic model. He was in principle, what he was by profession, a Protestant Episcopalian. I make this remark emphatic, because his hearty sympathy and co-operation with evangelical christians of all churches, have sometimes given rise to the suspicion—a suspicion which has been even publicly expressed—that he was not fully loyal to the church he served. He held that there was nothing in his relations as an Episcopalian, inconsistent with his higher relations as a Protestant and a Christian—nothing which compelled him, for a form or a rite, "a baptism or a laying on of hands" to unchurch and hand over to "uncovenanted mercies," millions of the living and the dead, who bore the seal of the Spirit. With the founders and earlier and greater lights of his own church—her Cranmers, and Ushers, and Burnets, and Taylors, and Leightons, and Halls, he held that Episcopacy was not a doctrine, but a fact; not of divine command, but only of apostolic example— the best, but not the only form; so that, while all are bound to accept it, the want of it does not necessarily, and of itself, exclude from the covenant. He believed that the visible church with its ministries and sacraments, was but a means of grace, not that grace itself; an instrumentality for diffusing the blessings of salvation, not that salvation itself. But he did not believe that the grace of God was inseparably incorporated with the church, nor that his truth and spirit were so tied to the episcopate as to be "of none effect" without it. External forms and rites, and orders and successions in the ministry, however necessary to the completeness, he did not regard as essential to the being of a church. In his view there was nothing incompatible between the ideas of a divinely appointed ministry, and a church which embraces all who believed the truth, and were sanctified by the spirit of God. Outside of the pale of episcopacy were thousands who gave ample evidence that they were partakers of the same grace, and heirs of the same promises as those within, and these he rejoiced to acknowledge as brethren. "Although,"—I quote his own words from a letter addressed to a Presbyterian Minister—"Although of another branch of the great family of our common Lord, I long to see the cause of true religion prosper every where; and while I could wish all you Presbyterian brethren were as I am, save these bonds of sin which hang around my own poor heart, I am yet content to wish you God speed in your own way; and to rejoice whenever, and wheresoever, and by whomsoever Christ is preached and souls brought home to God." In the language of one who speaks by authority here, "matters of ecclesiastical arrangement and government were esteemed by him within

the privilege of individual choice, and were not en-
grafted into the essentials of christianity itself. He
respected the preferences of others, and claimed the
same for his own, in the matter of form and order,
but he belonged, by the grace of God, also, to that
heaven destined body which his own church defines
as "the Holy Catholic Church, the communion of
saints, which is the blessed company of all faithful
people." He occupied the broad Protestant platform
where we stand side by side to-day, in perfect consist-
ency with his own principles, and in the full integrity
of his heart. His professions of fraternal regard to-
ward all, of every name, who bore the imprint of
his Master's image (professions so often suspected
and suspicious, so often but the cloak of selfish and
sinister designs) were the genuine and unaffected ut-
terances of his heart. Everywhere, in the pulpit,
on the platform, in ecclesiastical conventions, he
maintained, consistently, and with unflinching firm-
ness, the broad principles of Christian Fraternity.
His name belongs to no sect or segment of the household of faith, it is the common inheritance of us all.
The whole "company of faithful people" honored him
living, and mourned for him dead, as the champion
of Protestant unity.

III. His sympathies overleaping all narrow denom-
inational limits, were wide as the world—wide as both
worlds. How largely were all our benevolent institutions, our House of Refuge, our Asylums, our In-
firmaries, indebted to his judicious counsels, and un-

wearied labors. "When the ear heard him then it blessed him, and when the eye saw him it bare witness to him, because he delivered the poor that cried, and the fatherless, and him that had none to help him; the blessing of him that was ready to perish came upon him, and he caused the widow's heart to sing for joy."

His heart was knit especially to those great twin institutions which unite all who love the Lord Jesus, in direct efforts to save souls. When he spoke of the Bible Society, or the Tract Society, his countenance always glowed, his tongue was always eloquent. He loved them for their works' sake. He loved them as the visible signs and symbols of christian unity, the broad banner of our common Protestantism flung to the winds, and rallying around itself all the divisions of the great army of salvation. He was present at the organization of the American Tract Society, in 1825, a scene which all who witnessed described as a foreshadowing of heaven—and to use his own language, at its recent anniversary, "From that day to this, I have felt it a privilege and a duty, in the pulpit and upon the platform, and upon every occasion in which Providence afforded me an opportunity, to advocate the claims of this Society, as one of the great movements in our Protestant cause; and I have looked upon it as spreading an influence over the general literature of our country, with which no other agency could begin to compare. Hence, I most cordially endorse the sentiments of Bishop McIlvaine, that if this Society were crippled in any way in its operations, it would be a day of darkness to our common Christianity ; a day of rejoicing to infidelity and Romanism, from one end of the land to the other." He believed with Dr. Archibald Alexander, when he said, "I doubt whether there is in the world at this time, an institution, the Christian Ministry excepted, more efficiently employed in conveying the Gospel to all classes of society." Next to the Ministry, both these sainted men regarded the Tract Society as the great instrumentality for evangelizing the world.

At the time of his death, Dr. Johns was the President of the Maryland Tract Society. "Dr. Johns," I quote the language of its Secretary, the Rev. S. Guiteau, in announcing officially his death, "has presided over this Society during the whole of its existence. It is now about fifteen years since the friends of this branch of Christian effort judged best to reorganize the Baltimore Tract Society, one of the oldest associations of the kind in the country, to enlarge the sphere of its action ; and assume the name it now bears. On that occasion it was made my duty to call on Dr. Johns, and ascertain if he was willing to become our President. His reply was characteristic, 'I would advise you to get a man better suited for the place, but if my services are desired, they shall be cheerfully rendered.' You will all bear witness how fully he has redeemed this pledge. From that day to this day of mourning, it has been both my duty and my happiness, often to call and confer with him as to what was wise and best to do. I have never found him so busy, or so fatigued, that he was not ready to listen to my statements. Nor was it a mere passing consideration that he gave to these interests; but an earnestness of thought, such as men are wont to bestow on their personal concerns. I have never conversed with a man who had a higher appreciation of this department of christian benevolence." His services, in organizing and presiding so long and so efficiently over the Maryland Tract Society, were invaluable; and his name will always be preserved among her most precious household treasures.

IV. And now we come to the last sad scene of all. His work here was done, and the Master had need of him for a more glorious service above. While he yet went in and out among us, we saw the handwriting of death upon him. A concealed malady was slowly drying up the fountains of life, and embalming his body for its burial. His soul was mellowing and ripening for Heaven, and bathing itself continually in the light of God's countenance. Ere yet he approached the dark border river, or felt its first ripples upon his feet, he was admitted—as is sometimes granted to Pilgrims—to "the Land of Beulah," that Heaven this side of death, and close upon its borders, where the birds always sing, and the flowers always bloom, and the sun shineth night and day, and the shining ones come forth and walk— he stood upon the Delectable Mountains, whence he could see the open gates of the Celestial City; and so strengthened and cheered by these glimpses and fore-tastes of the Better Land beyond, he was enabled to go forward, singing that blessed Psalm of faith: "Yea though I walk through the valley of the shadow of death, I will fear no evil: for thou art with me; thy rod and thy staff they comfort me."

His last sickness, he knew from the first, was the Messenger of Jesus to call him home. His sufferings were intense and protracted, till his poor body was weary with its groanings, and its tossings to and fro; but his soul was kept in perfect peace; for God was the strength of his heart, and his portion. Come let us gather around his death-bed and see how a Chris-tian dies. He is looking back over his past life, and thinking of that world he must so soon leave, but there are no regrets; for his language is "I am now ready to be offered, and the time of my departure is at hand; I have fought a good fight; I have finished my course; I have kept the faith; henceforth there is laid up for me a crown of righteousness." His weep-ing family are around him; the memories of dear absent friends come crowding fast upon him; but he shrinks not from the stroke which must sunder so many tender ties at once; for he knows his Heavenly Father will take care of the bleeding hearts he leaves behind, and all will soon be reunited, never, never to part again. He sees death, the last dread enemy, approaching nearer and nearer; but even as he looks, the monster is suddenly transformed into a Messenger of Mercy, his crown of terrors falls off, his dart is broken, his sting withdrawn, and the dying saint sings, "O! Death where is thy sting? O! Grave where is thy victory? Thanks be unto God who giveth us the victory through our Lord Jesus Christ." He looks down into the grave just opening at his feet, but it is no longer a cold, or dark, or silent, or lonely place. It is a hallowed spot—Jesus lay there. His father lies there, his mother, the dear friends of other days, Patriarchs, Prophets, Apostles, all the sainted dead, and he is ready to lie down and sleep by their side. He looks upward; and his countenance becomes radiant, his filmy eye sparkles with more than its old lustre, the anticipated radiance of Heaven surrounds him as a glory; for he sees his Saviour beckoning him away; and with glad voice he answers—they were among his last words—"Yes, Jesus, I come! I come to thee!" It would seem, as if like the dying Stephen, he saw Heaven opened, and the Son of Man standing at the right hand of God, calling and beckoning him away.

On his death-bed he left these three legacies. The first is for that people he loved and served so well in the Gospel. Said he to those who stood around him: "I CANNOT EXPRESS THE PLEASURE IT HAS BEEN TO ME TO SERVE THIS PEOPLE; THEY HAVE BEEN SO KIND, SO CONSIDERATE." The second is for us all. It was in his last night on earth. His sufferings were intense, and he had thrown himself across the bed, with his face downward. His brother, Bishop Johns, was by his side, holding his hands; while a beloved son pillowed his head. The windows were thrown open to the night to give him air. Controlling his sufferings for a moment, by a strong mental effort, he looked up, and said in a clear calm voice to his brother, "Brother! it is all as clear as a sunbeam, and so comforting." Racked with pain; his face bowed to the earth; amidst the darkness of midnight; his only comfort the cold night winds that swept over him; it was noonday in his soul, for Heaven's own sunbeams filled and flooded its chambers. The third, too, is for us all. A few hours before his death, he said to those who watched around him, "Before my mind leaves me, I wish to say three things. I commit my family to the care of my Heavenly Father—knowing that he will do far more than I have ever been able to do for their protection; that I leave my Church to the guardian care of Almighty God; and that you must tell my friends, I am a sinner saved by grace, and that God my Saviour has not forsaken his poor servant in his dying hour." And so he fell asleep, calmly peacefully, as an infant sinks to slumber.

> "He died, as sets the Morning Star, which goes
> Not down behind the darkened west; nor hides
> Obscured among the tempests of the sky,
> But melts away into the light of heaven."

And then, devout men came and carried him to his burial. That funeral, who that witnessed, can ever

forget it. It seemed as if this whole city were draped
as a funeral mansion, and every inhabitant came
forth as a mourner That densely crowded church;
its death-like stillness, broken only by the stifled sobs
that could not be suppressed—the multitudes who
thronged all the surrounding streets—the long pro-
cession—the crowded cemetery—the tears which con-
secrated the last resting place of one so loved. Hallowed spot! The footsteps of undying affection will
often revisit it. Our hearts will often make their
pilgrimages there. Softly may the sunlight sleep
upon it; and fresh and green be the turf that covers it.

And now, farewell! Brother, farewell! With
trembling hands we have woven this garland for thy
grave—would it were worthier. We bless God that
we were permitted to know thee. We bless God
that we were worthy to love thee. Very pleasant
hast thou been unto us, my brother! And now that
thou art gone from us we will cherish all that thou
hast left to earth. We will watch over thy grave.
We will keep thy memory fresh and fragrant in our
midst. We will embalm thy name in our heart of
hearts. We will try to follow thee, brother! even as
thou didst follow Christ. Just translated from among
us; even yet we are standing and gazing after the
chariots of fire which conveyed thee away. O! that
thy mantle may fall upon us!

Why linger any longer about his grave. "He is
not here, he is risen."

"Hark! the golden harps are ringing
Sounds unearthly greet his ear:
Millions now in Heaven singing,
Greet his joyful entrance there."

He was wise to win souls unto Christ, and he shines to-day as the brightness of the upper firmament! "He turned many to righteousness," and he will shine "as the stars for ever and ever." The crown he wears to day is all sparkling—gemmed with immortal brilliants—the souls he won to Jesus. The mansion he inhabits to-day is very near to the throne; many were waiting to meet and rejoice with him there, and many more will yet go up to join them, and a great multitude will gather around him over whom he will rejoice forever as "his crown and his joy," and "his works will still follow him."

A word I must say in parting, to the Officers and Members of the Maryland Tract Society. A dear personal friend, a brother beloved—an honored President, "our stay and our staff," has been taken from us in the noon of manhood, and in the very midst of his usefulness. We shall never see his face more—never again meet him in the Committee-room. But a voice comes from his grave to us saying, "Be ye also ready, for in such an hour as ye think not the Son of man cometh. Work while it is day, for the night cometh when no man can work." O! how rapidly that night is hastening on, and how soon it will close around us. How many of those who started out on life's journey with us—the friends and companions of other days—have fallen at our side, and are sleeping to-day in some quiet country church-yard, or in our own crowded cemeteries. Already we begin to feel ourselves "strangers in the earth." And what we have to do for our own souls, for the souls of- others, for that precious Saviour who redeemed us with his own blood, must be done quickly.

Here, in this solemn hour, and as over the remains of our dear departed friend and brother, let us consecrate ourselves afresh to that great cause whose precious interests are entrusted to our guardianship. We bless God, that here, though bearing many a name other than that new name we shall all be known by in Heaven, we see eye to eye, and are joined hand to hand, "laborers together" in building up our Master's Kingdom. Let us ever cherish that spirit of brotherly kindness, which so eminently characterised our lamented President, and which glows in our hearts to-day. Let us not be weary in well doing. Let us scatter abroad still more widely the leaves of the tree of life—the printed words of God—till they bring healing to all the dwellings of our City and State. And when the Chief Shepherd shall appear, we too "shall receive from him a Crown of Life."

APPENDIX.

CHARGED by the Managers with the duty of having the fore-going Sermon issued from the press, I have taken the liberty of adding the subjoined documents in an Appendix to the Second Edition, without the trouble of convening the Board to ask its sanction. Of the acceptableness of these documents to those with whom the memory of Dr. Johns is so precious, there can be no doubt, and as no responsibility is devolved upon any one but myself, I am confident of the approbation of the Managers.

Cor. Secr'y.

TRACT HOUSE, Fayette street,
June 15, 1859.

Extract from the forthcoming Annual Report of the American Tract Society, of which Dr. Johns had been an exceedingly influential Corporate Director for many years, and by whom it was most nobly represented on the platform of the London Tract Society, at its anniversary in 1852.

The Rev. HENRY VAN DYKE JOHNS, D. D., of Baltimore, who for eight years has been a Director of this Society, and for fifteen years President of the Maryland Branch, departed this life April 22, 1859, at the age of fifty-six.

Dr. Johns early imbibed the friendship of the late Rev. Dr. Milnor, was present with him at the organization of the American Tract Society, and continued its cordial active friend and supporter not only during the twenty years that Milnor lived, but through thirty-four years till they were called to meet before the throne above. None present at the Society's last anniversary will fail to remember the Christian kindness and courtesy with which he addressed that meeting.

"It was my privilege," he said, "to be at the meeting in 1825, when the Society was organized, and I never shall forget the tone, sentiment, and emotion which pervaded that whole assembly. If there ever was an occasion when the Spirit of God, of love, of concord, and a sound mind was poured out, it was upon that occasion. I recollect seeing venerated men bathed in tears, and weeping like children in sympathy, heart with heart, as the plans and prospects of this institution one after another were presented. And, Mr. President, from that day to this, I have felt it a privilege and duty, in the pulpit or upon the platform, and upon every occasion in which Providence afforded me an opportunity, to advocate the claims of this Society, as one of the great movements in the Protestant cause, and I have looked upon it as spreading an influence over the general literature of our country, with which no other agency could begin to compare. Hence I most cordially endorse the sentiments of Bishop McIlvaine, that if this Society were crippled in any way in its operations, it would be a day of darkness to our common Christianity, a day of rejoicing to infidelity and Romanism from one end of the land to the other."

The Board of the Maryland Branch Tract Society, at a meeting the day after Dr. Johns' death, unanimously

"*Resolved*, That this Board have heard with feelings of deepest sadness of the death of their highly esteemed and much loved President, Rev. H. V. D. Johns, D. D.

"*Resolved*, That in this solemn and painful bereavement, which an all-wise Providence has visited upon us, we would recognize the hand of our heavenly Father, would bow with meek and humble submission to his will, and acknowledge that he 'doeth all things well.' The Board desire to record their high estimate of the character and usefulness of their much loved associate. As their President, he has rendered the Society most valuable service; his sound judgment, active efforts, his extensive influence, and above all, his earnest piety, warm-hearted Christian love and fervent philanthropy, all combined, made him most useful to our cause, and attached him to every member of this Board with almost the affection of a brother. They would bear testimony to his enlarged and liberal views, to his singleness of purpose in promoting the cause of Christ—the highest welfare of his fellow-men, uninfluenced by personal or sectarian interests, seeking only to win souls to salvation, and to promote the glory of the Redeemer's name. His elevated Christian character as a minister of Christ, his kind, sympathizing spirit, gentleness of manner, and mildness of disposition, were characteristics that rendered him influential as a man of God, valuable as a citizen, and beloved by all who knew him. We feel that the church of Christ has lost a faithful minister, our community a most valuable citizen, our Society and influential and devoted friend and President, and ourselves as individuals an attached friend."

At this meeting of the Board of the Maryland Branch, the Rev. J. W. M. WILLIAMS, of the Baptist church, Chairman of their Executive Committee, said :

"I should do violence to my feelings if I did not say something before taking the vote on these resolutions. There is no man living I love more, in a religious sense, than I loved Dr. Johns. I said this while he was living; I say it now he is gone. We have labored together in this Society for the last eight years. My acquaintance with him has been of the most pleasant and profitable character. I scarcely ever met him but he uttered some word that made me love him more, and cheered me on in my work of preaching the gospel.

"In former years, while we as a Society were struggling under difficulties, he was our guiding spirit, and his counsels were always wise and safe. We shall miss him greatly. His death comes near to me ; I feel it deeply. He being Chairman of the Board of Managers and I of the Executive Committee, we have alternated in presiding over the deliberations of this Society. As I stand here this afternoon in the place he filled with so much pleasure to us all for fifteen years, I feel as if a fellow-soldier had been shot down at my side, and I had stepped up to fill his place, and perhaps the next ball may reach my heart. Let us all lay his death to heart, and hear our common Master saying to us, 'Work while it is called to-day.' 'Be ye also ready.' "

The Rev. S. Guiteau, Secretary of the Maryland Branch, said on the same occasion:

"There is not a member of this Board, I might almost say there is not a religious man in Baltimore, who has not heard with feelings of deepest sadness that the Rev. H. V. D. Johns, so long the beloved President of this Society, is numbered with the dead. Yesterday morning, at about six o'clock, he passed away from earth. His last words were, as if called to, 'Yes, Jesus, I come, I come to thee.'

"Dr. Johns has presided over this Society during the whole of its existence. It is now about fifteen years since the friends of this branch of Christian effort judged best to reorganize 'The Baltimore Tract Society,' one of the oldest associations of the kind in the country, to enlarge the sphere of its action, and assume the name it now bears. On that occasion it was made my duty to call on Dr. Johns, and ascertain if he was willing to become our President. His reply was characteristic: 'I would advise you to get a man better suited for the place; but if my services are desired, they shall be cheerfully rendered.' You will all bear witness how fully he has redeemed his pledge. From that day to this day of mourning, it has been both my duty and my happiness often to call and confer with him as to what it was wise and best to do. I have never found him so busy or so fatigued that he was not ready to listen to my statements. Nor was it a mere passing consideration that he gave to these interests, but an earnestness of thought such as men are wont to bestow upon their personal concerns. I have never conversed with a man who had a higher appreciation of this department of benevolence.

"He loved the Society as an efficient agency for proclaiming to men of all grades their ruin and their remedy. I speak what I know when I say that he specially delighted in the declaration of the late Dr. Alexander, of Princeton, a man whom he greatly revered, in his letter resigning his place on the Publishing Committee, and quoted by Bishop McIlvaine in his speech at the last annual meeting: 'I doubt whether there is in the world at this time an institution, the Christian ministry excepted, more efficiently employed in carrying the gospel to all classes of society.'

"He loved the Society also, peculiarly loved it, because it tended to promote the unity of the church. How he loved to talk of the meeting when the Parent Society was organized, and when 'Milnor, Summerfield, and others,' to use his often repeated words, 'manifested a spirit so much like heaven, that the recollection of it is refreshing.'

"You all remember how we were impressed with his remarks at our Colporter convention last autumn. We shall not forget that memorable declaration:

"'I love these associations, assemblages such as these, composed of members of various branches of the church. They serve to counteract that sectarian zeal to which we are so prone—a spirit of which I am so afraid that for years I have made it a habit not to pass a place of worship of another denomination without lifting up a silent prayer that God would bless that people.'

"Happy spirit! How congenial to that world where he now is, where names are lost, and Christ is all and in all!"

Extract from the Records of the Maryland Bible Society.

"At a special meeting of the Board of Managers of the Maryland State Bible Society, held on the 23d instant, the following preamble and resolutions were unanimously adopted:

"*Whereas*, It has pleased Almighty God, by the dispensation of His providence, to remove from this transitory life Rev. HENRY V. D. JOHNS, D. D., and whereas the deceased was for a number of years a member of the Maryland State Bible Society, therefore,

"*Resolved*, By the Managers of the Maryland State Bible Society, in special meeting assembled, that we entertain and hereby express our high appreciation of the Christian meekness, devotion, usefulness, and truly Catholic spirit of Rev. Henry V. D. Johns, D. D., and that our associations with him, in the circulation of the Holy Scriptures, greatly endear him to us, as an able, intelligent and constant supporter of the Bible cause.

"*Resolved*, That we sincerely sympathise with the bereaved family of the late Rev. H. V. D. Johns, D. D., and also with his afflicted parishioners, to whom he was a faithful Minister of the Lord Jesus; and that we commend them to the Chief Shepherd, for the consolation and support of Divine grace.

"*Resolved*, That a copy of the above proceedings be furnished to the family of the late Rev. Henry V. D. Johns, D. D., to the Vestry of Emanuel Church, and that they also be published in the newspapers of this city."

Signed by order of the Board,

O. H. TIFFANY,
Recording Sec'y.

Extract from the Records of the Young Men's Christian Association.

ROOMS OF THE YOUNG MEN'S CHRISTIAN ASSOCIATION OF BALTO.,
Saturday Evening April 23, 1859.

At a special meeting of the Board of Managers, the following resolution was unanimously adopted, as expressive of the sense of that body:

Resolved, "That in the death of the Rev. HENRY VAN DYKE JOHNS, D. D., the Young Men's Christian Association of Baltimore, has sustained a loss so great, that its Board of Managers cannot withhold expressions of its grief.

"The Board is deeply sensible that it has been deprived of a friend, whose mature judgment, wise counsel, and godly example greatly contributed to the advancement of its truest interests, and of one whose name was a 'tower of strength,' in securing the christian fellowship, which unites the various denominations of this city.

"The Board desires to mingle its heartfelt sympathy with his family, which has been so sorely bereaved, and earnestly prays that the 'God of the fatherless and the widow' may abundantly administer to them the peace and the consolation of His Holy Spirit.

"To his afflicted congregation also, would the Board extend its condolence, and devoutly pray that God in his infinite mercy, may send 'a man after his own heart,' who will 'know nothing but Christ and Him crucified,' to guide His people in the way of life everlasting."

J. DEAN SMITH, *President.*

JOHN R. KELSO, Jr., *Rec. Sec'y.*

TRACT HOUSE, FAYETTE STREET, *June* 14, 1859.

To THE VESTRY OF EMANUEL CHURCH :

Gentlemen :—A second edition of Dr. Smith's Sermon Commemorative of the Life and Character of your late Rector, the lamented Rev. H. V. D. JOHN, D.D., is called for. As almost every item of authentic information, and every utterance of affection relative to this beloved man seems to be craved by the Christian public, I have thought the pamphlet would be rendered more valuable as a memorial of Dr. Johns by the insertion, in an Appendix, of a few other documents called forth by his death. Among others, your Minutes adopted at the announcement of his decease, seems to me eminently appropriate. For this purpose I solicit a copy from your records.

With high esteem and the sincerest sympathy, I am, gentlemen,

Very truly, yours,

S. GUITEAU,

Cor. Sec. Maryland Tract Society.

To Members of Vestry, care of
H. A. THOMPSON, ESQ., *Register.*

BALTIMORE, *June* 15, 1859.

To the REV. MR. S. GUITEAU,

Cor. Sec. Maryland Tract Society :

Rev. and Dear Sir :—Your letter of 14th inst. to the Vestry of Emanuel Church has been received, and I have been desired to hand you a copy of the proceedings of the Vestry consequent upon the death of our late much beloved and revered rector, the Rev. HENRY V. D. JOHNS, D.D., which you will receive with this note.

With much respect, yours, very truly,

H. A. THOMPSON, *Register.*

EMANUEL CHURCH VESTRY ROOM, }
Baltimore, 22d April, 9 o'clock, A. M. }

THE Vestry met. Present: The Rev. Charles R. Howard, *Assistant Minister.* Messrs. James Carroll, Henry A. Thompson, Henry M. Bash, Leonard Mackall, Haslett McKim, William Bose, Robert Dorsey of Ed., and James H. Millikin.

Prayers were offered by the Assistant Minister.

The Assistant Minister communicated to the vestry the sad intelligence of the death of our beloved rector, the Rev.

HENRY VAN DYKE JOHNS, D. D. He fell asleep in Jesus, at six o'clock, A. M., this 22d day of April, 1859.

Whereupon, it was

Resolved, That a committee, consisting of Messrs. Carroll, Thompson and Bash, be, and the same is hereby appointed, to convey the heartfelt condolence of this afflicted vestry to his afflicted family: to claim the mournful privilege of sympathizing with their sorrows, and affectionately to ask them to unite with us in seeking consolation under their and our sad bereavement, in the full assurance that our loss is his everlasting gain.

Resolved, That the committee be instructed to confer with the family on the order of the funeral and to tender the services of the vestry in any and every way in which they will consent to receive the same.

Resolved, That the following address to the congregation be adopted.

From the Vestry to the Congregation of Emanuel Church, Baltimore.

It has pleased Almighty God to take our beloved Rector home. He died as he had lived, trusting in God his Saviour, and praying for us all.

The earthly ties which bound him and this congregation together are severed: he has gone to his eternal rest, and we are left to mourn our sad bereavement.

In our deep distress it becomes us to bow our heads in the dust, and to say, "Even so, Father, for so it seemed good in thy sight."

But there are ties which death cannot sever. Henry Johns is embalmed in our hearts.

The man, the Christian, the Minister of the Word and Sacraments lives in our tenderest affections. And although we shall no more receive at his hallowed hands the memorials of a Saviour's dying love, no longer look upon his beaming countenance, and hear the silvery tones of his voice, directing us to Christ, as the Way, the Truth, and the Life, we shall retain a constant preacher of the blessed gospel in the Godly example of his holy life and conversation.

Our dear brother is not dead. He is still a living member of the Holy Catholic Church, the Communion of Saints, which is the blessed company of all faithful people.

> "Angels and living saints and dead
> But one communion make,
> All join in Christ their vital head,
> And of his love partake."

He has only left the Church militant to take the place prepared for him in the Church triumphant. And it is our blessed privilege to know and feel that we may receive health and salvation only in the name of our Lord Jesus Christ.

Let us, then, take our place at the foot of the cross, in the assured hope and trust that there is a place prepared for us, even for us, unworthy as we are, if we also be found faithful to the end; and that we shall again unite with him in ascribing glory to the Father, and to the Son, and to the Holy Ghost, not in an earthly sanctuary, but before the throne of God and the Lamb.

Resolved, That a copy of these proceedings be forwarded to the family of our late Rector, and that they be read to the congregation on the first occasion of public service.

Eight o'clock, P. M.

The Vestry met by adjournment.

Present all the members.

Prayers were offered by the assistant minister.

The committee appointed this morning reported, That they have had an interview with Mr. Henry Johns, to whom they delivered a copy of the proceedings of this morning's session, which had been previously read to the congregation at morning prayer—this day being good Friday. They learned from him that the family had directed an advertisement in the public papers announcing the death of Dr. Johns, and inviting his friends to attend the funeral at Emanuel Church, on Sunday, at 3 o'clock, P. M. That the family desired as much privacy as was practicable, and wished that the assemblage at his late residence should be confined to his immediate relatives. They desired that the members of the vestry should act as pall bearers, and should attend at his house at half past two o'clock, for the purpose of accompanying his remains to the church, and to the grave. They desired to have the usual funeral services, without a sermon, and wished the services to be conducted entirely by the Rev. Mr. Howard.

These directions, given at the express wish of our late Rector, should be a law to the Vestry.

Their duties will then be confined to an endeavor to accommodate in the best way they can, those who attend at the church.

On motion,

Resolved, That the report be accepted, and the Vestry cheerfully acquiesce in the wishes of the family, that the Rev. Mr. Howard perform the funeral services, and that they attend at the residence as pall bearers at the hour designated.

Resolved, That the Vestry wear crape on the left arm, and that the church be put in mourning for the space of one month.

Resolved, That the Register be, and he is hereby authorized to give such directions for the carriages, &c., as may be necessary.

BALTIMORE, 25th *April,* 1859.

The Vestry met.

Present all the members.

Prayers were offered by the Assistant Minister.

The committee reported, That having learned from Mr. Howard that it was the desire of the family to make some change in the order of the funeral of our late Rector, have thought proper to address to him the following letter:

BALTIMORE, 24th *April,* 1859.

REV. AND DEAR SIR:—The Vestry had matured a plan for the order of the funeral of our beloved Rector, in strict compliance with the expressed wishes of his family. That plan contemplated your performance of all the funeral services.

We have learned this morning that the family desire the association with you of the Rev. Mr. Hoff in the performance of those services.

It is not our province to interfere in any way with your ministerial functions. But we desire to say to you, that, as at first, so now, the wish of the family is a law to us; and that you have our sanction for any alterations they may desire to make.

Very respectfully and affectionately yours,

JAMES CARROLL,
HY. A. THOMPSON,
H. M. BASH,
Committee of the Vestry.

Rev. CHARLES R. HOWARD,
Ass't Minister Emanuel Church, Baltimore.

The committee further reported, that at half past two o'clock on the 24th instant, being Easter Sunday, the Vestry attended at the residence of our late Rector, where they received his sacred remains and accompanied them to the church. They found the church filled to its utmost capacity.

We bore the coffin through a wave of suppressed sobs, testifying the heartfelt love and veneration of the congregation, tempered by a profound respect for the place and the occasion.

We deposited it in front of the chancel, when two of our members removed the Bible and Prayer book from the desk, and placed them directly over that heart in which they had been so long enshrined.

After the services, which were performed by the Rev. Messrs. Howard and Hoff, all that was mortal of Henry Johns was for the last time taken from that church he so fondly loved, and laid in the grave, there to await the Resurrection. We close as we began—"Even so, Father, for so it seemed good in thy sight."

On motion the report was adopted.

[Certified extract from the records of the Vestry of Emanuel Church, Baltimore.]

HENRY A. THOMPSON, *Register.*

A Letter from the Vestry of St. Paul's Church, Cincinnati, Ohio, to the Vestry of Emanuel Church, in this city.

[COPY.]

At a meeting of the Vestry of St. Paul's Church, Cincinnati, held on the second Monday after Easter, 1859, it was, on motion,

Resolved, That the Rector, the Rev. Dr. Greenleaf, and Messrs. D. K. Cady and S. W. Pomeroy, be a Committee to take suitable notice of the death of the Rev. HENRY V. D. JOHNS, D. D., late Rector of Emanuel Church, Baltimore, and for several years Rector of St. Paul's, Cincinnati, Ohio, and to communicate the same to the family and parish of the deceased.

In the performance of this duty, the Committee can only repeat the tribute which has elsewhere been spontaneously offered to the purity of character, the affectionate sympathy, and untiring zeal in all good works, of this departed minister of Christ, and most respectfully and kindly offer to his bereaved family the assurance of our sympathy in their sorrow, and to the parish from which he has been removed, our sincere condolence on this afflictive dispensation of God's providence.

P. H. GREENLEAF,

D. K. CADY,

S. W. POMEROY,

Committee.

A very admirable writer in the Episcopal Recorder of May 7th, referring to conversations with Dr. Johns, when topics were discussed likely to induce censorious remarks, says:

"I felt as if I stood in the presence of one who was so far receding from earth as to lose sight, in the atmosphere of love which encircled him, of all but those grand and dear relations which bind Christians to each other as the common servants of a crucified Lord."

He concludes his notice as follows:

"The last time I heard Dr. Johns preach was on Thanksgiving day last. He had just risen from an attack of sickness. That this sickness had brought him, not merely very near to death, but very near to heaven, was impressed upon me not merely by the appearance of his body, but by the working of his mind. There was an *etherealness* in the way in which his subject was treated, which spoke of one whose thoughts were now much more conversant with things spiritual than with things temporal. The topic was of a thanksgiving character, but the thanksgiving was one for eternity rather than earth. Three months afterwards, when I again met him, and spent some time with him this impression grew deeper. Three months more passed, and death stood at the very door of his mortal tenement, announcing, in unmistakeable language, his approach. But the messenger came to him not by surprise. That calm preparation which had been proceeding so long and so gradually was not ruffled by the knowledge that in a very short time probation was to end. And then, in three weeks more, that probation did end in peace.

"Dr. Johns' death is the greater loss to the Church, from the fact that his mature and gentle wisdom, and his wide charity, now beginning to be the more fully understood, are qualities which our present wants peculiarly require. 'God buries his workmen,' was an epitaph prepared by John Wesley for his brother Charles, 'that he may carry on his work.' Let this be our comfort, and let us unite in the prayer that to fill the place of him who has been taken, others may be called to do the work of the Lord with increased energy and meekness."

From the Baltimore American of 22d April.

THE Rev. HENRY VAN DYKE JOHNS, D. D., Rector of Emanuel Church, of the Protestant Episcopal denomination, died this morning, a few minutes after six o'clock, at the family residence, corner of Bolton and Lanvale streets. For a week previous the press of the city had announced the fact that the Doctor was extremely ill, and daily thereafter continued to report the progress of the disease. A year ago, the deceased experienced a similar attack, and for several days was prostrate, but under judicious medical treatment recovered, and resumed the active discharge of his ministerial duties. Nearly two months since, however, he experienced symptoms of the same indisposition, but continued his clerical labors until the middle of March, at which time, with the advice of the vestry of the Church, and the members of his own family, he was constrained to resign his work to the assistant of the parish, Rev. Charles Howard, and submit to medical treatment.

Soon after, the family physician, Dr. John Buckler, was called in, and at once pronouncing his disease of a dangerous character, treated it with unusual skill and watchfulness. The frequent changes in the condition of the patient, sometimes enabling him to leave his bed and converse freely with the assistant rector, his family, and the vestry of the Church, than whom all others were positively forbidden to see him, seemed to justify anticipations of his final recovery, but it was otherwise decreed. On last Monday, the Right Rev. John Johns was summoned from the active discharge of the duties of the Episcopate of the Diocese of Virginia, and soon appearing at the bedside of his brother, never left it until the vital spark had fled.

Extract from the recent Address of the Rt. Rev. Bishop Whit-TINGHAM, "To the Seventy-sixth Annual Convention of the Protestant Episcopal Church in Maryland."

"We are again warned to diligence and faithfulness in our work by the presence of death among us since our last assemblage. A name that had stood, with the exception of a comparatively brief interval, for upwards of thirty years upon the roll of the Clergy of the Diocese will appear there no more. Prematurely, as it might seem to man, certainly in the very height of activity and usefulness, the Rev. HENRY VAN DYKE JOHNS, the beloved and influential Rector of Emanuel Church in this city, has been taken from his family, his ardently devoted flock, and a whole mourning city. His extensive connexions and long residence in the diocese had made him one of the most generally known of all our band. His winning manners and earnest zeal for the service of his Master, secured the respect of all, the love and admiration of such as were more intimately associated in his work. Probably none among us, when called to rest, would be missed and mourned by so many. Long years must pass before the void which his departure makes in the ministry of Baltimore can be so supplied as to appease the sense of grievous loss, now filling so many hearts with anguish. Eulogy of such a man would be out of place, on this occasion. To you, the mere mention of the deceased is his ample praise."

———

The following beautiful tribute from the distinguished Pastor of the Fifth Avenue Presbyterian Church, New York, will be read with great pleasure.

From the Presbyterian.

MESSRS. EDITORS.—Though very much unfitted for literary work by a low state of health, I cannot refrain from sending you a few paragraphs concerning my honored and beloved friend, the late HENRY VAN DYKE JOHNS, D. D. That he belonged to a different branch of Christ's Church from that in which I serve, has always added zest to our friendship and fraternity. So many years have elapsed since the events which are presently to be related, that I feel like one who speaks concerning strangers, or persons very remote; they are indeed events which I never expected to disclose to the public.

The first person with whom I ever talked freely, respecting the infinite concerns of my soul, was Henry V. D. Johns; and he has told me that a like remark would be true of himself. It was in Nassau Hall, then the principal edifice of Princeton College; and in No. 27, the "second entry;" a locality fresh in the memory of old Nassovians. We were boys of sixteen; though I was about to commence bachelor of arts. Such conversations begin, one scarcely knows how; in a short time we had unbosomed ourselves to one another, and entered upon a close and tender friendship which I trust in God is never to cease. During the days in which Henry was under the work of the law, and humbly doubting whether indeed he had attained to justification or not, he used to walk in the grove behind the college, which, alas, with other forest shades of my boyhood, has long since vanished away. As he strayed, musing, his eye was attracted by a small folded paper upon the ground; this he picked up, and afterwards showed to me; it contained these words: "And they that are Christ's have crucified the flesh with the affections and lusts, Gal. v, 24. *Try yourself by this!*" This incident made a deep impression on us both, carrying to our apprehensions at that time something of the supernatural. We have talked it over in later years, and there is reason to believe that it had a moulding influence on Johns' experience and life. Soon after this we became communicants at our respective homes.

In the survey of many brethren whom it has been my exceeding great privilege to know during thirty odd years of ministry, I can recall none who "followed" the Lord "fully" (Numb. xv, 24,) in a higher sense than Henry V. D. Johns. He was not a great genius, a man of extraordinary erudition, a famous author, or a pulpit-phenomenon; but he was a faithful, fervent, and most successful minister of the Lord Jesus. Great honesty, transparency, directness, thoroughness, intrepidity, earnestness and melting affection, characterized his words and acts. He was a man of heart, always glowing; for, so far as I could discern, the fire never went out. This made him truly and powerfully eloquent, as he uttered just such doctrines and exhortations, as those of Bickersteth, Ryle, and McGhee. The catholicity of his spirit was great, and savored of the nobler days of the Church of England. Equally remarkable were his courage and independence, in resisting ecclesiastical domination. Such a union of manly force and feminine gentleness showed how closely he had followed the Master.

In the summer of 1844, a slight steamboat disaster caused me to stop, with my family, on Saturday evening, at Newcastle, where we became the guest of Henry's distinguished brother, Chancellor Johns. These were hospitalities never to be forgotten. On this occasion we were presented to the father of the three justly honored sons, the venerable Judge Johns, then more than eighty years of age. A few days after, at Cape May, all three brothers met, and I sat beside another friend of my boyhood, Bishop Johns, who, I am quite sure, will forgive the allusion. That most delightful of seaside resorts was made

thrice blessed by such company of scholars, gentlemen, and be-
lievers. Many an innocent, but keen rejoinder, passed between
the two Episcopalians and the two Presbyterians. I had not
met Henry for many years, and we became boys again, as we
rehearsed the scenes of beautiful Princeton along the resound-
ing strand of cool Cape May. Everything now confirmed me
in my judgment, respecting those traits of Henry's character,
which I have ventured to note above—his incorruptible truth,
his contempt for all indirectness and finesse, his genuine liber-
ality in church matters, his boldness, and his triumphant love.

On the 22d of July, he gave a discourse in the Methodist
Church, from Ezek. xxxiii, 11, "As I live, saith the Lord God,
I have no pleasure in the death of the wicked," &c. It was
delivered without notes, and was a sermon among a thousand,
if measured with reference to the real ends of preaching, being
true, correct, fluent, warm, and above all, full of *unction ;* this
is the word which characterizes Johns' preaching. It was the
doctrine of the Reformers, the Articles, and the Homilies;
sound, evangelical, cogent. I never heard that voice again in
public, till it rang forth its affectionate warnings, just a year
ago, at the Anniversary of the American Tract Society. On
the 28th of July, Bishop Johns preached at Cape May, from
Jer. ii, 19.

These lines have been penned before I could receive any but
the most general account of dear brother Johns' death. The
papers tell, indeed, that on the arrival of the Bishop, he said,
"Brother John, here is a sinner saved by grace!"

I wish these hasty sentences were not so egotistical; but any
attempt to make them less so would have impaired their sim-
plicity. In conclusion, I will not say with Shenstone's cele-
brated epitaph, *Heu quanto minus cum reliquis versari, quam
tui meminisse!* because I see and feel that I am surrounded by
many ministers, and other beloved servants of our Lord; but
I will add, in remembrance of my youth : *I am distressed for
thee, my brother Johns; very pleasant hast thou been unto me !*
2 Sam. i, 26.

I am always faithfully yours,

JAS. W. ALEXANDER.

Dr. Newton's estimate of Dr. Johns' Character.

Extract from a letter of Rev. Richard Newton, D. D., of Philadelphia, to H. A. Thompson, Esq.

"Many thanks for the excellent funeral discourse delivered by Dr. SMITH on the occasion of the death of Dr. JOHNS. It is a beautiful analysis of his lovely character. I was so much interested in it that I read it to my people in place of the usual lecture on last Wednesday evening. Every body was delighted with it, and many inquiries have been made for copies of it.

"I hope the Tract Society that has published it will send a supply to the Tract Depository here."

THESE several extracts I have collected as so many flowers culled from the wide field of Christian affection, and strewn them upon the new made grave, mementos of fifteen years of harmonious companionship in benevolent effort, and of a friendship, the recollection of which is precious to my heart.

I may be permitted to add, in the words used by Dr. Alexander, not "in remembrance of my youth," but of my riper years, "I am distressed for thee, my brother Johns; very pleasant hast thou been unto me." 2 Sam. i, 26.

S. GUITEAU.